Little Hedgehog Goes to School

Rhea Pechter

For Leo, Zach, & Ruby

Library of Congress Control Number: 2022909452
Paperback ISBN: 978-1-7327459-1-9

As soon as the sun slipped behind the hill, Little Hedgehog leapt out of bed.

She made herself a yummy breakfast of snails and mushrooms.

She went to her hat closet
and gazed at all of her hats.

She had one for every occasion.

Now she needed a hat
for the biggest occasion of all.

PERFECT!

Perfect for my very first night of school.

DING!

Mmkay.

I can't wait to cross the bridge over the river!

And there will be a **SHOOTING STAR** shimmering across the—

There is no bridge on the way to school.

And there will probably not be a shooting star.

Well...

I'm really looking forward to when they give me my school cape—the one with 'LH' on the back in bright gold letters. In the picture I drew the other night, all the students had school capes. The capes are magical and they let you fly around like birds.

Dad realized what was going on.

He was used to Little Hedgehog's big imagination.

Little Hedgehog's big imagination was very powerful, and very delightful, but also—sometimes—not so helpful.

There are no ponies at school.

I'm certain there are.

I'm certain there are not.

How can you be so sure?

TIME TO GO, DAD!

Little Hedgehog.

Yes?

You can't wear a hat to school.

Are you sure?

Yes.

Little Hedgehog put the hat back in her closet.

On the way to school, Little Hedgehog
looked ahead to see the bridge.

She kept looking and looking,

but soon she and
Dad were standing right
in front of her school.

Hmm...no bridge.
No shooting star.

Inside, Little Hedgehog's teacher showed her where to put her things.

She had her own cubby with her name on it.

Is it...Little Heedgehog?

Actually, it is Little *Hedgehog*.

Oh! I'm sorry. Let me show you to your carpet square.

LITTLE HEDGEHOG

Little Hedgehog grinned as she envisioned her beautiful, special carpet square.

Here you are.

But all of the carpet squares were plain and blue.

Hmm...

In class, they sang songs

and read books

and drew pictures.

Later, they all walked in a line down the hallway to music class. Little Hedgehog looked around, excited to get a glimpse of the ponies—especially her pony...

But there were no ponies.

The rest of the night, Little Hedgehog looked for all of the things she'd imagined so clearly.

She couldn't find any of them.

When it was time to go, Little Hedgehog
retrieved her backpack from her cubby.
She waited at the door.

Behind her, another little hedgehog was waiting.

Her name was Bebe.

Have you seen any ponies?

I am a pony.
NEIGH.

Oh!

I am a pony, too.
I'm a purple pony.

NEIGH!

I'm a sparkly blue pony
named PICKLE.

Little Hedgehog, her dad, Bebe, and Bebe's mom all walked home together.

Bebe stopped at a little mound of dirt on the way.

Little Hedgehog, come up on the bridge with me. Look at the shooting star.

Little Hedgehog ran to stand with Bebe
on the little mound of dirt.

They jumped up and down as they
gazed up at the dark night sky.

Back in the burrow,
Little Hedgehog climbed into bed.

Good morning, Dad.

Good morning, Little Hedgehog.
Have a good sleep.

I have a best friend now.

I noticed.

Tomorrow, Bebe and I will fly around in our magical capes.

I'm sure you will.

Dad kissed Little Hedgehog's paw and left, just as the sun crested the hill.

Made in the USA
Las Vegas, NV
20 October 2022